Through the Rainbow

Indigo Book 2

In the Park

by E. S. BRADBURNE

Illustrated by *LESLEY BELLAMY*

SCHOFIELD & SIMS LTD., HUDDERSFIELD

There is a park
at the end of Simon's street.
Elizabeth and Simon play in the park.
They play ball and they play catching
in the park.
They are taking Spot with them.
You must be good, says Elizabeth,
or we will not let you come with us.
You must not run away.

There is a pond in the park.
Simon is taking his boat
to sail on the pond.
He has put it on the water.
Look, he says, look at my boat.
Can you see it, Elizabeth?
Can you see my boat in the water?
There are some children
playing by the pond.
Look at my boat, Simon says to them.
Look everybody, I can make my boat sail.

Look, Simon, says Elizabeth.
Spot is going into the pond.
Look out for your boat!
Come out, Spot. Come out, good dog.
I must get my boat, says Simon.
Help me to get it, Elizabeth.
Quick! We must not let Spot have it.
Come and help me to get it out
or Spot will have it.
I am going to paddle in for it.

You will fall in, says Elizabeth.
You will fall into the water
and get your clothes wet.
I will not get my clothes wet,
says Simon.
I will not fall in.
I am going to paddle.
Spot is coming out, says Elizabeth.
He is coming out over here on this side.
He is all wet.
The water is going all over me.
He is making me all wet.

He has got weed all over him.
Look at the pond weed, all over Spot.
Help me to get it off him, Simon.
The weed is all wet.
He must run and get dry.
He must not go back to the house
all wet.
I can dry him with some grass
and get the weed off him.
Help me to get up this soft grass.
It is good to dry him with.
Come here, Spot, and let me dry you
with this soft grass.
Now make him run, Simon.
Come on, Spot, run and get dry.

I am going to take off my shoes
and paddle, says Simon.
I am going to take off
my shoes and socks
and paddle in the pond.
Come and paddle with me.
Take your shoes off,
it is soft on the grass.
I am going in here, follow me.
I am going to paddle too,
says Elizabeth.
Let me come in with you.
We must not paddle in the weed.
Come in over here,
there is no weed on this side.

Look out, Simon, Spot is taking your shoes,
says Elizabeth.
He has got them.
He is taking them away.
Run and catch him, Simon. Quick!
He is running away with your shoes
Naughty Spot!
Hurry up! We must get them back.
Simon and Elizabeth
are running after Spot.
He is taking Simon's shoes to the pond.
Will he put them in the water?
Can they catch him first?

Spot has put the shoes down on the grass
by the pond.
He has not put them into the pond
after all.
Good Spot! You are a good dog,
says Simon.
You did not put my shoes in the water.
I did not have to paddle in for them.
I did not have to get them out
of the pond,
and they did not get wet.

There are some ducks on the pond.
There are six ducks.
Look at the ducks, says Elizabeth.
Can you see them, Simon?
I can count them. There are six of them.
Look at them.
They are coming over here to us.
They are hungry.

The children have some buns for them.
Simon has a bag of buns
and Elizabeth has one too.
They are going to give them to the ducks.
Here they come, says Elizabeth,
all six of them.
Quack, quack, come here ducks,
says Elizabeth.
I will give you some of my buns.
I like ducks.
Simon will give you some buns too.
Come on, come here.
Quack, quack, quack.

I am going to give the ducks my buns,
says Elizabeth.
Are you going to give them your buns too,
Simon?
Look at me throwing the buns to them.
They do like them.
They are all coming over to us,
all six of them.
They are catching the buns,
can you see them?
Good ducks, quack, quack, quack.
I am going to give you all
some of my buns.
You are all hungry.
Here are some buns for you to eat.

Look,
the ducks are coming out of the water.
Look at their wings, says Elizabeth.
Can you see their wings, Simon?
Look, they are going to fly.
All the ducks are going to fly.
They have big wings.
There they go.
Look at their wings.
Did you see them go?
Did you see their big wings?

Come and play house now, says Elizabeth.
I am going to have a house under here.
I am going to make it under this tree.
It is dry here on the grass.
Would you like to come in my house?
I will let you come in too.
It is a secret house. Do you like it?
You can have a house next to it.
You can have a secret house too.
Here is a dry house for you
under the tree.
We can hide in the secret houses.
There are good places to make houses
in the park.
There are good secret places.

There is a house for Spot too,
under the tree.
Can you make him go into it?
I will make a bed for him in his house.
Here is some soft dry grass for his bed.
Come on, Spot,
here is a soft dry bed for you.
Spot will not come into the house.
He does not like it.
He would like to play.

Come on, run, says Simon.
I will catch him.
Come on.
Look, I can catch Spot.
Run, Spot, good dog, run.
Spot is running round the pond
and Simon is running after him.
Spot can see a puppy.
It is a little soft puppy.
He is going to play with it.
The puppy is running away.
He does not like Spot.
Spot is too big.

The puppy is going into the pond.
It is going to fall in.
It will go in the weed.
We must get it out, says Elizabeth.
Hurry Simon.
Quick! We must get it out of the water.
I will paddle in and get the puppy out,
says Simon.
I can get it.
Here it is, Elizabeth.
The puppy is all wet,
and Simon is all wet too.
Simon and Elizabeth
will have to dry the puppy
and Elizabeth will have to dry Simon.

Simon has got a top to play with.
He can make it go round fast.
Look at my top, says Simon.
Look everybody. It is going round fast.
Can I play with your top?
says Elizabeth.
Let me have it. Let me have a turn.
I can make it go round.
Look, I can do it too.

Can you see the circles in the grass?
says Elizabeth.
They are all over the grass.
Can you see them?
They are magic circles.
The fairies made them, she says.
They made them by putting magic dust
on the grass.
No one can see the fairies working.
They do it when no one is about.
It is all a secret.
This is one of their secret places.
You can come into the circles, Simon.
You must take off your shoes first.
It is magic here.
What would you like to have?
Count to 100
and the fairies will give it to you.

I am going to climb this tree,
says Simon.
I can climb the tree by myself.
Look at me.
Can you see me up here?
Can you see me at the top of the tree?
It is good up here.
Come down, Simon, says Elizabeth.
You will fall.
I like it up here, says Simon.
I will not fall.
I can see all the park.
I can see the pond
and I can see the houses.
I can see my house too,
and I can see the children down there.
I can climb to the top of this tree.

Come down, Simon, says Elizabeth.
Mummy would not like you
to be up the tree.
She would make you come down.
I am coming down, says Simon.
Look out, I am coming down fast.
I am an aeroplane with big wings.
I am going to fly down. Here I come.

Come and play hide and seek,
says Elizabeth.
You go and hide first
and I will come and look for you.
It is your turn to hide first.
Quick, Simon, you go and hide.
I will hide my eyes and count 100.
There are good secret places to hide
in the park.
It is good for playing hide and seek.
I am going to hide my eyes now.

The children are playing hide and seek.
They are going to hide in the long grass,
and Elizabeth is going to look for them.
This tree is home, says Elizabeth.
I am going to hide my eyes and count 100.
Now I am coming.
The long grass is good to hide in.
Elizabeth will not see them there.
The park is good
for playing hide and seek.
There are good places to hide.

It is Simon's turn to hide.
Hide your eyes, he says to Elizabeth.
He is going to hide by a tree.
It is a big tree.
Elizabeth will not see me here, he says.
It is Elizabeth's turn to seek.
She is counting to 100.
Coming! she says.
She is going to find Simon.

Elizabeth has to look all round
for the children.
She can see Simon by the tree.
I can see you, she says.
Now it is Elizabeth's turn to hide.
You must seek me now, she says,
and I will go and hide.
You must hide your eyes and count 100.
You must come and find me.
It is my turn to hide now.
You must not look.
I can find secret places to hide.
No one can find my secret places.
Hide your eyes, Simon.

I am going to climb up there,
says Simon.
Look at me, I can climb to the top.
It is good up here.
I can see over the top.
Simon, come down, says Elizabeth.
You must not climb up there.
You will fall.
Quick! There is a man coming.
Get down Simon,
or he will make us go away
and he will not let us come
into the park.
Quick, come down, Simon.

There is a little train in the park.
It is for the children.
There is an engine and six coaches.
It is a little silver engine.
The train is at the station.
Simon and Elizabeth and the children
are on the train.
The signal is down.
The driver is making the engine go
and the wheels are going round.
The train is going into a tunnel.
I like going on this train,
says Elizabeth.
I like going on it too, says Simon.

Look, the duck*s* have come back,
says Elizabeth.
Are they all here?
I will count them.
All the six ducks have come back.
They are all on the pond,
all six of them.
They are down on the water.
They are all in the weed.
They are coming to us for buns.
They are hungry.
My bag is empty now,
all my buns are finished.

I am hungry too, says Simon.
We must go back for tea now.
We must go home.
I would like some buns and jam for tea.
Come on, we must run back.
Quick, Elizabeth, we must go home now.
I am hungry too, says Elizabeth.
I would like some cake for tea.
Will there be cake for tea
when we get home?
Put your shoes and socks on, Simon,
says Elizabeth.
Have you got your boat and your top?
Take them with you.
Come on, Spot,
we are going back for tea now.
Hurry up, we are going home.

The children are going home
for their tea.
They are going to tell mummy
all about what they did in the park.
Elizabeth will tell mummy
about the six ducks and the puppy.
Simon will tell mummy
about going up the tree.
Elizabeth will tell mummy
about playing hide and seek
in the long grass,
and Simon will tell her
about the little train.